HOPELESS HEROES

ARACHNE'S GOLDEN GLOVES!

STELLA TARAKSON

Sweet Cherry PUBLISHING

Published by Sweet Cherry Publishing Limited
Unit 36, Vulcan House,
Vulcan Road,
Leicester, LE5 3EF
United Kingdom

First published in the US in 2019
2019 edition

2 4 6 8 10 9 7 5 3 1

ISBN: 978-1-78226-552-8

Hopeless Heroes: Arachne's Golden Gloves!

Cover design by Nick Roberts and Rhiannon Izard
Illustrations by Nick Roberts

www.sweetcherrypublishing.com

Printed and bound in India
I.TP002

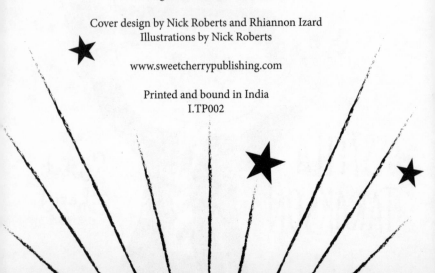

For Peter,
for everything

"Make sure you wear your scarf." Mom bustled into Tim's room as he finished getting dressed for school. Even though it was spring, she was wearing her winter coat. "It's freezing again. Wish I could just stay home today."

Tim wished she could too, or at least that she could be back when he returned from school. It wasn't much fun coming home to an empty house. It had felt even worse since his good friend Hercules had returned to his home in Ancient Greece.

"I can't. It's wrecked, remember?"

Mom hadn't believed Tim when he'd said that the scarf had unraveled itself. But what else could he say? She hadn't taken him seriously when he'd told her about Hercules, who'd been trapped in their old Greek vase by the wicked goddess Hera. Mom almost certainly wouldn't believe what had happened next. By grabbing onto the vase, Tim had unwittingly traveled to Hercules' home. Tim had been wearing the scarf at the time. It wasn't his fault it had got caught up in the action.

"That's right, I was going to get you a new one. I forgot. Sorry, but I've had … uh … other things on my mind. Important things. Look, Tim, I've been meaning to talk to you about this. I shouldn't put it off any longer ..." Mom's cheeks flushed red and a fine sheen of sweat covered her face.

Tim thought he knew what she wanted to say. He nodded and smiled reassuringly. "Is the furnace acting up again? Don't worry, Mom. Just get a man in."

Mom gulped and spluttered. "Funny you should say that. You see, I ..." She cleared her throat, paused, and shook her head. "There isn't time for this now. I want to do it properly. How about you show me the scarf and I'll see if it's wearable?"

Tim handed it over and Mom frowned. "No, it's too far gone. Toss it out. But put on your gloves at least."

"They're too small. Remember? You said you'd get a new pair."

Mom's face brightened. "Oh yes! Your grandma knitted you some. I'll go get them."

She left the scarf behind and Tim hastily crammed it in a drawer. He didn't want it thrown away. It was a souvenir of his adventure and a reminder of his encounter with Theseus the Minotaur Slayer. Theseus had unraveled the scarf in a futile attempt to escape the labyrinth that Hera had trapped them in. In the end, Tim had been the one to find the way out.

"Here." Mom came back in and handed him a pair of brown gloves. "Try them on."

They were much too big and were made out of coarse yarn.

"They're scratchy," Tim complained.

"They'll have to do for now," Mom said, fastening the belt on her coat. "I'm off. Make sure you wear them on your way to school. We don't want you getting chilblains again. Bye, dear."

She gave Tim a quick hug, left his room … and screamed.

"What? What happened?" Tim bolted after her. He had never heard his mother scream like that before. It was a scream of sheer terror, as if there were a kill-you-with-a-glance gorgon after her.

"A sp-sp-spider …" Mom stuttered as she pointed at the wall. "Big."

Tim followed her shaking finger and, sure enough, a large spider was clambering along the hallway wall.

"Get a broom, quick! I'll keep watch to make sure it doesn't hide.

URGH!"

Tim darted down the corridor and came back with a broom, a glass, and an envelope. He'd taken the opportunity to remove the scratchy brown gloves and thrust them in his jacket pocket.

"Whack it! Hard. Hurry before it jumps on us!"

Tim didn't want to hurt the spider, so he nudged it gently with the bristly end of the broom. It fell to the floor and his mother leaped back. Acting swiftly, Tim slapped the glass over it, taking care not to squash it.

"It's okay, Mom, I've caught it."

She shuddered. "Kill it! Urgh, it's horrible."

Tim looked down at the hairy brown spider trapped in the glass, waving its long legs frantically as it tried to climb up the slippery sides. The poor thing hadn't done anything to hurt them. It was just crawling along, minding its own business. He couldn't bring himself to kill it.

"I'll take it outside," he said, bending down and sliding the envelope under the glass.

"Don't you dare. It'll come back inside. Just … squish it or something."

Tim had never realized his mother had such a vicious streak. He flashed her a severe look. "I'll take it down the street and let it go. It won't come back." Not after hearing his mother scream like that. The poor spider was probably scarred for life.

"It better not," Mom grumbled. She leaned forward to kiss him like she usually did, then backed away nervously. "See you tonight. And then we've got to talk."

Tim carried the spider to the end of the street, being careful not to jolt it. The spider stared up at him through the glass, bright eyes gleaming. Tim rather liked

the idea of keeping it as a pet but knew his mother would go nuts. "Sorry about this," he murmured. "Nothing personal." The spider waved its front legs as if it understood.

"Talking to a glass now, are ya, Cinderella? Next you'll be talking to a teacup." It was Leo the bully, who seemed to have made it his life's mission to make Tim miserable. The unkind nickname was a jab at the fact that Tim had to help out with housework.

Tim and Leo had crossed paths the day before, when they had both been dragged around a boring garden center. Leo had tripped Tim up and Tim had returned the favor. It had felt good at the time. Great, actually. But now that they were alone in an empty street, with Leo clenching his beefy fists, Tim thought it probably wasn't the wisest thing he could have done. If only Hercules were still with him, he'd frighten Leo off again. But no.

This time, Tim was on his own.

"HOW ABOUT I SMASH THAT STUPID GLASS?"

Leo said, thrusting his freckly face close to Tim's. "Or maybe I should smash your stupid nose instead. Whaddya reckon?"

Tim thrust the glass near the bully's face. "How do you like my new pet? I was taking it for a walk before school."

Leo recoiled, his face aghast, before quickly recovering his composure. Hands on hips, he put on an I-don't-care expression. "It's all right. I s'pose." He sniffed, but eyed the glass with respect. "What sort of spider is he?"

"Actually, it's a she. The females are bigger than males. And more dangerous."

Tim had no idea what type of spider it was, but using his imagination had never been a problem for him. Guessing that Leo wouldn't know anyway, Tim invented something impressively dangerous. "She's an Australian howling widow spider. They're called that because they howl after a kill. See her powerful fangs?" He thrust the glass closer and Leo blinked.

"Is … is she deadly?"

"Of course. But that's okay. I've trained her not to bite my friends."

Leo's eyes widened. "What's her name?"

Tim said the first thing that came to mind. "Hera." It seemed fitting to name her after the dangerous goddess who had trapped him in the labyrinth.

"Do you often take her for walks?"

"I try. She gets restless if I don't. Last week she killed a rat because she was bored."

Leo took an involuntary step backward. "Dude, have you ever thought of getting something normal? Like a dog or a cat?"

"Nah." Tim shook his head. As much as he'd love a real pet, he knew they couldn't afford one. Still, he wasn't about to admit that to Leo. "Hera would get jealous and kill it."

Leo blanched, which made the freckles on his face stand out more clearly. "Can … can I hold her?"

Tim couldn't help feeling a grudging respect for the bully. Most kids would turn and flee. Whatever else could be said about Leo, there was no doubting his courage. "Sure. Hold the envelope under the glass, or she'll climb on your arm."

Gulping, Leo held out his hands. They were shaking and Tim could see the effort the bully put into steadying them. He also noticed how swollen his fingers were. Purplish red and raw, the skin was pulled tight over the knuckles. It was even blistered in places. "What's wrong with your hands?"

Leo's expression instantly hardened. "Nothing." He stepped away and thrust his hands behind his back.

Tim thought he knew. Chilblains. He often got them in winter, but nowhere near as badly as Leo. Maybe that was because Mom made Tim wear gloves when he left the house. He wondered why Leo wasn't wearing any.

Balancing the glass and envelope carefully with one hand, Tim reached into his jacket pocket and pulled out the scratchy

brown gloves his grandmother had knitted. He shrugged and held them up. "Here. These are too big for me."

Competing expressions chased each other across the bully's face. Anger, embarrassment, gratitude. Resentment. He stared at the gloves, lips pressed into a thin, hard line, and didn't move.

"Go on, take them." Tim waggled them in the air. "I don't want them."

Leo opened his mouth to reply, but the words died on his lips.

Not meeting Tim's eye, he snatched the gloves and stalked off in the direction of their school.

Tim watched until Leo was out of sight before placing his pretend pet on the footpath. "I have to let you go now," he said to the spider, lifting off the glass. "Sorry to bring you out in the cold, but you know what mothers are like. It's better than being squashed, though."

The spider agreed. It reared up on its hind legs and waved its front legs, enjoying the feel of fresh air on its fangs. Its bright eyes sparkled in the morning light, and Tim thought he detected gratitude in its gaze. It was staring up at him as if he were a hero.

A lump formed in Tim's throat. He didn't feel like a hero ... not since he'd left the gorgon's victims to their fate. Since returning from Ancient Greece yesterday, Tim couldn't stop thinking of the people the gorgon had turned to stone. He wished he could go back and help them.

Maybe he could! A spell written on the old Greek vase suggested that Tim could order it to take him anywhere. It had certainly worked when he'd commanded it to bring him home after his

recent adventure. But that had been in Greece, where the vase's magic might have been stronger. Would it work here, too? Could he order the vase to take him back to Ancient Greece? There was only one way to find out.

The spider turned and scuttled under a shrub as Tim ran back home, his fingers crossed.

Tim eased the sheet-covered vase out of his wardrobe, where he kept it hidden. He pulled the sheet off and looked at the fracture lines crisscrossing the vase's surface. Tim had glued the vase back together after accidentally breaking it and at first he'd felt bad about the damage. Mom had wanted to sell the vase, which would have brought in enough money to allow her to quit her second job. After it was broken and repaired, however, Mom had said no one would be willing to pay much for it.

"Thank goodness," Tim murmured. If Mom had sold the vase, Tim would never have had his amazing adventure. Even worse, Hera might still have been able to track the vase down. She could have stolen it from the new owner – who probably wouldn't have been expecting ancient gods to break in. Then Hera could have used it to recapture Hercules.

The mantel clock in the living room chimed, reminding Tim that it was time to go to school. Feeling torn, he paused. He wanted to go back to Ancient Greece as soon as possible. The

thought of those poor people turned
to stone by the gorgon was gnawing
at him. He knew he wouldn't be able
to concentrate on his lessons properly
until he'd tried to rescue them.

But … maybe he could go now.
Yesterday he'd returned from a whole
day in Ancient Greece to find that
only a few minutes had passed in the
present. Hopefully that would happen
again. Besides, Tim was anxious to
check that the vase's magic would work
for him in the present day. It was awful
to think he might never see his new
friends again.

"Oh vase," he intoned, gripping its
handles, "take me to Hercules' house."

Lucky he'd remembered to hold on tight, because he immediately felt himself flying through the air. A feeling of elation filled him. Yes! It was working!

Just like last time, an impenetrable golden mist swirled around, making it impossible for him to see. Tim closed his eyes and waited until he felt himself land on solid ground. Holding his breath, he hoped the vase had taken him to the right spot. What

if it had gone back to Hera's temple instead? He would be delivered right into her hands!

Tim opened his eyes and let out his breath. It was all right. The vase had taken him directly to Hercules' front door. He eased it onto the ground and rolled his aching shoulders. The vase was bulky, and clinging on to it like that was tiring.

"What are you doing here?" a familiar voice behind him asked.

Spinning around, Tim saw Hermes walking in his direction. He had wings on his cap and sandals, and they flapped gently as he moved.

"I – I came to visit."

"Not smart. You don't want Hera to know you're here." Although he was a god, Hermes worked as Hera's servant. He seemed calm and cool when the queen goddess wasn't around, but in her presence he cringed and bowed and scraped as if he were terrified.

"She doesn't have to know," Tim said, touching the vase protectively. "I'm not going anywhere near her."

"She'll know. She'll sense the vase's presence."

Tim blanched. He hadn't thought of that. "I'll keep it safely in Hercules' house. That should be okay, shouldn't it?"

But Hermes was shaking his head, his golden curls catching the sunlight. "She'll know it's there. Listen." He leaned forward, his eyes solemn. "Give it to me. I'll make sure she doesn't find it."

"Well …" Tim wasn't sure. How did he know this wasn't a trick? After all, Hermes was the one who'd given the vase back to Hera in the first place.

"I know what you're thinking," Hermes said. "Can you trust me?" He winked.

"COURSE YOU CAN!

31

I only obey Hera when I have to. What she doesn't know won't hurt us, know what I mean?"

Tim was still hesitant.

"Look. How's this for a sign of good faith?" The young god waved his hand over the vase. As if by magic, all the fracture lines disappeared. The big black vase was as good as new! Smooth and glossy, it looked fresh off the potter's shelf.

"WOW."

"You can say that again." With a swift

movement, Hermes picked up the vase. "Don't you worry about a thing, Tim Baker. I'll look after it. Come see me when you want it back." He started walking before he finished talking.

"I WANT IT NOW!"

Tim bustled after the god. "I need it to get back home."

Coming to a halt, Hermes cocked his head to the side. "I'm keeping it safe for you, little buddy! What's your problem? Would you rather Hera gets it?"

Tim gulped. "No."

"Do you wanna be stuck here forever?"

"Of course not."

"Then leave it with me." Hermes flashed a winning grin. "Hera will never suspect that *I'm* hiding it."

That kind of made sense. Maybe the young god was right. "Where will I find it?" Tim called out.

"My temple," Hermes shot back. "Easy to find." And then he – and the vase – disappeared.

"Are you crazy?" Tim's friend Zoe's eyebrows shot to the top of her forehead. "Why did you give Hermes the vase?" The vexed girl looked a lot like her father, Hercules. Although Tim would never say it, she acted like him too. Zoe had inherited the hero's love of adventure and a disdain for anything that tried to stop her. Luckily for her, though, she had inherited her mother's intelligence rather than her father's.

Tim shifted his weight from one foot to the other. "I didn't give it to him. Not exactly. He just kind of … took it."

Home alone, Zoe had answered the door when Tim knocked. Hercules had gone out to visit his hero friends, and his wife Agatha was at the well collecting water and catching up on town gossip. Zoe had taken Tim upstairs into the gynaikon, the women's sitting room. Men weren't allowed in such rooms, she'd explained, but as Tim was still a boy, it was okay.

He'd looked with interest at the colorful tapestries decorating the walls, but Zoe didn't give him a chance to explore the room further. Once she'd realized that the vase was missing, she sizzled with bad temper.

37

"You know he works for Hera! What if he's handed it over to her? She'll use it to catch Dad again!" Her eyes flashed with frustration.

"I – I'm sure it's fine. He's the one that warned me about Hera." Tim sounded more confident than he felt. "And he fixed the vase up too, good as new. I'm pretty sure he was only trying to help. Without Hera around he seemed quite nice, actually." Or so Tim hoped.

Zoe groaned and face-palmed. "He's the god of thieves and liars! I've told you that before. You can't trust anything he says.

HE LIES FOR A LIVING!"

"Err … can I sit down?" The couch didn't look too comfortable but he felt awkward standing around.

"Yes. No. We need to get the vase back first."

Tim sat anyway, thinking about what Zoe had said. "I don't think we need to panic. You said your dad's not alone. Even if Hera *has* got the vase, she can't do anything yet. Not if he's with other heroes." Zoe didn't look convinced, so Tim continued. "There's just one thing we need to do first, and then we'll go get the vase. I promise."

"What?" Zoe remained standing, arms folded across her chest.

Tim explained that he couldn't stop thinking about the gorgon's victims. All it had taken was one glance at snake-haired

Stheno's face, and they'd been turned into statues. With the help of vain Theseus, Tim and Zoe had managed to defeat the gorgon. The danger was over, but Stheno's victims were still frozen in stone. "We've got to help them. We can't just leave them like that, with tears running down their cheeks."

Some of the fire went out of Zoe's eyes and her voice softened. "You're right. What do we do?"

"Let's go back to the garden. We can ask your great-great-grandfather for help."

Zoe's ancestor was Perseus who, in his time, had been one of the greatest heroes in Ancient Greece. Many years ago he had cleverly worked out how to slay Medusa, another gorgon, without being turned to stone. Now he spent his retirement years in the gorgon's garden, where he tended the flowers with fanatical care and devotion.

"If he knew what to do, he would have saved them himself," Zoe said, perching on the edge of a chair.

"Maybe." Tim didn't want to criticize the old man who seemed more interested in

flowers than hero work. "But it won't hurt
to ask him for ideas."

. . .

"Two visits in two days," cackled Perseus
when Tim and Zoe approached the garden.
"That's more than in the last few decades."

"Hello, Grandpa." Zoe dashed over
and hugged the frail old man who was
hobbling around with a walking stick.
She took care not to trample on

any of the flower beds. Tim nodded a
greeting then veered off to examine one
of the crying statues. It was a young man,
crouching forward as if he were trying
to run, a horrified look on his face. Tears
continued to trickle from his eyes. Tim
dabbed them away with a balled-up tissue
he found in his pocket.

"Can't get enough of my petunias, eh?"
the old man said.

"They're lovely," Zoe agreed. She looked at the rows of flowers in a way that made Tim suspect she didn't know which were the petunias. "Grandpa. We were wondering whether you know how to help these poor people." She gestured around the garden at the figures frozen in stone. "Is there any way to undo the damage?"

"What's that?" Perseus cupped his hand to his ear. "You want to un-statue them?" He shook his head. "I wouldn't worry about that. They're quite happy here, admiring my garden every day. What could be nicer? No, I just let them enjoy the view."

"They don't look too happy–" Tim started to say, but Zoe shushed him.

"Yes, but if they come back to life they can tell you how splendid your flowers are," she said. "I'm sure they'd love that opportunity."

Perseus stroked the scraggly gray hairs of his beard. "True. I hadn't thought of that. Well, there's one thing you could try."

"What's that?"

"I can't promise anything, mind you. I don't have any personal experience of it, you understand. But I have heard tales of a powerful object with remarkable healing properties."

That was more like it! Tim gave the statue an encouraging pat on the arm, then walked up to the old hero. "What object?"

"I've long considered using it for marigold mildew, but I haven't been able to track it down." Perseus sighed. "If you find it, will you let me use it too?"

"Yes," Tim said, his excitement growing. "What is it?"

Perseus leaned on his walking stick and squinted across at Tim. "Child, have you ever heard of the

GOLDEN FLEECE?"

Tim did remember reading about the Golden Fleece. Something about an expedition across the sea to recover a magical sheepskin guarded by a dragon.

"Jason and the Argonauts, wasn't it?" Tim asked. "They got the fleece."

"That's right, child," Perseus said, peering at him closely. "You might dress strangely, but you're not as foolish as you look."

Tim looked down at his school uniform and made a mental note to ask Agatha if she could find him some Ancient Greek clothes. They'd help him blend in better and make it harder for Hera to track him down. But first things first.

"Do you think Jason will let us borrow the fleece?"

"Tell him I sent you," Perseus said. "If he refuses, say I'll cancel his order for a dozen red roses. That'll shake him."

"Thanks, Grandpa. How do we find him?"

Tim and Zoe listened as the old man gave them directions. Tim noticed Zoe's eyes widen when she learned they were to pass Hera's temple.

"Isn't there another way?" Tim asked, hoping to keep as far away from there as possible.

"No. Now off with you. I've got some important puttering around to do." Perseus shooed them away. "Let me know when you've got the fleece."

Tim wondered whether the crying statues understood that help was coming. He peered into the face of the one nearest him and fancied that he caught a flicker of hope in his stony gaze. "We'll be back soon," he said, "to make you good as new."

"Come on." Zoe was keen to start their quest.

They walked in silence, each lost in their own thoughts. Tim was obsessing over whether Jason would let them borrow the fleece. Maybe he wouldn't trust kids he didn't know with such a precious object. It wouldn't be at all surprising. Tim didn't know what Zoe was thinking – but he soon found out. Just as they were passing Hera's temple, Zoe abruptly changed direction. Without a backward glance, she bolted up the steps and into the goddess' courtyard.

"HEY!"

"I've got to see if the vase is here!" Zoe shouted over her shoulder. She passed between the columns at the temple's entrance and disappeared into the shadowy interior.

Tim kicked at the ground in irritation, stirring up a cloud of dust. Part of him wanted to leave her behind and continue on his way to Jason's house, but he knew he couldn't leave her alone to face the goddess. Scowling, he ran up the stairs after her.

Zoe nearly knocked him over on her way back out. "It's not there."

"Great. It shows Hermes didn't give it to Hera after all!"

"Does it? I don't know." Zoe shot a dark look at the temple. "They might be keeping the vase somewhere else so we can't find it."

"Or maybe Hermes was telling the truth. Maybe he really is trying to help us."

"Maybe." Her reply was grudging.

"Anyway, we'd better get going. We don't want Hera to know–"

Before Tim could finish his sentence, a horrible yowling filled the air. Hera's peacocks! The goddess had a flock of surprisingly aggressive birds that guarded

her temple. Their screams had a nasty tendency to summon Hera herself.

"RUN!"

Tim and Zoe fled down the rocky path. Tim had never run faster in his life and his lungs felt as if they would burst. They didn't stop running until they had left the temple far behind and were standing on Jason's doorstep.

"I think we got away with that," Zoe said, hands on hips as she gasped for breath.

"Yeah. Maybe."

Tim didn't say what was worrying him. Even if Hermes hadn't betrayed them, the peacocks' calls might be

enough for Hera to realize that Tim was back. Thrusting the thought out of his mind, he knocked on Jason's door.

There was no reply.

He tried again. "Don't tell me he's not here. After all that! Now what do we do?"

Zoe put a finger to her lips. "Shush. What's that noise?"

A banging sound was coming from behind the door, increasing in intensity. Tim tried pushing the door and it opened easily. He and Zoe walked into a courtyard and found a young man busily attaching a plank of wood to what looked like the prow of a boat. His dark hair was cropped very short all over his head, except for a long tuft on top that was slicked back

with hair oil. It slid over his face as he hammered away. At his feet was an array of tools.

"Are you Jason?" Tim asked, stepping forward.

"Hand me that rope, will ya?" The young man didn't look up as he held out his hand. Specks of sawdust were scattered all over his chiton.

Tim picked up a long piece of rope and placed it in the man's grasp.

"Mmpf." He grunted his thanks and kept on working.

Tim tried again. "I said, are you Jason? Of the Argonauts? We've been sent to find you. We need to ask a favor."

"Gimme that piece of wood."

Tim had to use both hands to lift it up. He didn't need to worry about splinters: although it was heavy, the wood was silky and smooth to the touch. "Here you are. It's just that we need to borrow the Golden Fleece. Perseus said we should talk to you about it."

"What do you think of this joint? Is it straight?"

Tim peered at it. "I think so." Turning to Zoe, he whispered, "Are you sure this is him?"

The little girl nodded vigorously. "I've seen him once or twice before. It's him."

"Mmm." Still not looking at them, Jason thrust his face closer to his handiwork.

Zoe was going pink in the face and Tim could tell she was about to pop with impatience. "Look," she snapped. "We need your help. Are you going to listen to us or what?"

Jason ignored her outburst. Zoe clenched her fists. The look in her eyes was exactly the same as her father's when he got cross. Tim signaled for Zoe to calm down. He knew how to handle this.

"Are you building a boat?" he asked Jason. "It looks great!"

The young man glanced at them for the first time, his brown eyes sparkling with delight. "Yeah, you think so? Thanks, bro! Who did you say you were?"

"I'm Tim Baker and this is Zoe. We need your help."

Jason didn't seem to be listening, though. "Bro, you like my boat? I've got these sick oars on deck, all hand-carved by me. They took weeks but" – he patted the boat – "Worth it! And look at the sweet shape of the stern. I reckon she'll go from 0 to 6 knots in under an hour."

Jason sounded like the car nut who lived next door to Tim. He was forever tinkering under his hood and revving the engine when he drove past. Sometimes Tim got stuck listening to him rant, which meant that Tim knew exactly how to handle this over-zealous hero.

"Wow! What are you going to call her?" He forced the enthusiasm into his voice.

Glowing with pleasure, Jason favored Tim with a grin. "Calling it the *Argonut*.

After my first ride the *Argo*, which got banged up in a race. Worst day of my life, that was."

"Sorry to hear that. So what's the buoyancy on her?"

"Glad you asked! It's gonna be better than my last ship, and that was nearly …"

The words blurred in Tim's mind, but he managed to nod and grunt in all the right places.

Simmering with impatience, Zoe nudged Tim in the ribs. "Come on," she hissed, "this is getting us nowhere."

Tim knew he had to break Jason's flow or else Zoe would barge in with all the tact of an outraged bull. That would be disastrous. People like Jason had to be handled very carefully or they simply shut you out.

"So, err, bro," Tim said haltingly, trying to get the words exactly right. "Can ya help us out?"

"What do ya need, my man?" Jason picked up a rag and wiped his hands with it. "You building a boat? Want a few tips?"

"Um, not at the moment. Some of my bros got turned to stone," Tim said, ignoring the look of incredulity that Zoe flashed at him. "Old man Perseus tells me you've got some mighty powerful fleece. Can you give us a lend?"

"Can't help you, bro. Sorry." Jason shook his head and looked back at his boat.

"Well then," Zoe snapped. "My great-great-grandfather – that's Perseus, if you didn't know – said to say that if you don't help, you can't have those red roses you wanted."

"Who's the chick?" Jason asked Tim, jerking his thumb at Zoe. "She's got enough hot air to sail the Aegean."

Tim suppressed a smile.

"How dare you talk about me like that! I'll have you know that I am Zoe, daughter of Hercules."

"Figures. You're just like him." Jason smirked, then looked back at Tim. "Tell you what, I'd love to help, you being a bro and all. But I can't. You see, I don't have that fleece no more. I gave it to my girl."

"Is that who you want the roses for?" Zoe asked, her attitude softening somewhat.

Jason snorted. "Course not. They're for my boat."

"So who's your girlfriend?" Tim

interrupted before Zoe could come up with a stinging reply. "Do you think she'll help us?"

"DUNNO."

The hero shrugged. "Haven't seen her in a while. You'll have to ask her. She's a real fit babe. Name's Arachne. Actually, her face would look cool on *Argonut*'s stern. I wonder if she'd pose for it? I know a good sculptor who'd do the job."

Tim gave up trying to talk like Jason. "If you tell us where she lives, I'll ask her."

Jason pointed. "Down that hill and turn left. Her place is the first on the right. And tell her to come and see my new ride."

"We will."

"Come on, *bro*," Zoe said, tugging at Tim's arm.

Tim waved goodbye to Jason, but the hero had already turned his attention back to the boat. It was only a short walk to Jason's girlfriend's house. Tim stopped at the front door. "What did he say her name was?"

"Arachne."

"Know anything about her?" Tim asked. Zoe shook her head.

"I hope she lets us borrow the fleece," Tim continued. "She might not, seeing as it was a gift. Maybe we can offer her some of Perseus' flowers as a thank-you present."

He knocked on the door. A peculiar scuttling sound came from the other side.

"Yes?" a muffled female voice demanded through the thick wood.

"Is this the home of Arachne?" Tim asked loudly so he could be heard. "We were sent by her boyfriend, Jason."

After a moment's pause, the door flew open. Tim's eyes widened in astonishment. Zoe let out a little scream and her hand fluttered to her mouth. Less than three feet away, a human-sized spider stood glowering at them.

"I'M ARACHNE. WHO'S ASKING?"

Zoe shrieked and tried to run away, but Tim gripped her elbow. He stared at the spider in fascination. She was huge. Five feet tall at least, from the tips of her glistening eyes to the feathery hairs on her feet. With fangs bigger than bananas and a glossy black body, she was an awesome sight. The only thing that was out of place was the frilly white apron tied around her waist.

"I said, who's asking?" Arachne repeated testily. She angled her head so that the sunlight reflected off her fangs.

"Sorry – wrong house!" Zoe said in a rush, lurching backward.

"No! I mean … hello. I'm Tim Baker and this is Zoe. Jason asked us to come and see you."

A hard expression entered the spider's eyes. It was doubly disturbing because she had so many of them: two large black orbs in the center of her face, with a row of six smaller eyes around the top of her head. Every single one of them flashed angrily.

"Jason! Humph. Is this for real? I haven't heard from him in months."

"He's building a boat," Tim said.

"Figures." Arachne snorted. "I'm surprised he remembers me. Boats matter to him more than anything."

It was hard to read the spider's facial expressions but Tim could tell from her voice that she was upset. If they were to have any chance of borrowing the Golden Fleece, they had to get on her good side. "He thinks of you a lot. I'm sure of it."

"Oh are you now?" she stepped closer, her voice tinged with menace.

Tim could feel Zoe trembling beside him and knew he had to pacify the spider. "Um yes. Jason wants you to pose for the figurehead. Because you look so fit, he said."

Arachne's head swayed thoughtfully. "Is that why you're here?"

"Partly," Tim said. "We also need to ask you a favor, and we'd be grateful if you could hear us out. Please."

The spider was silent for a moment. "Aren't you scared of me? Most children are terrified." The hairs on her legs quivered as she waited for their reply.

"NOT AT ALL!"

Tim shook his head vigorously. "I love spiders, honest. I rescued one just this morning."

"And what about her?"

A stiff smile crept across Zoe's face as she clutched Tim's hand. "M-m-me too. I'm not scared."

Arachne peered closely at the children before making up her mind. "All right. Come into my parlor." She scuttled backward and made room for them to

enter. Tim looked inside curiously. Like
Zoe's and Jason's houses, the front door
opened straight onto an open courtyard.

Across the center stretched a gigantic
spiderweb. Droplets of dew sparkled on
the silky strands, breaking the sunlight up
into miniature rainbows. Scenes of battles
and heroic quests were woven into the
shimmering strands. Tim had never seen
anything so beautiful in all his life.

"Mind the web.
It took me ages
to make that,"
Arachne said,

leading them to a wooden bench. "You
may as well sit. I can't ... not anymore."
Instead, she lowered her bulbous body
closer to the ground and looked at them
expectantly.

Tim found it hard to believe that Jason could actually be dating a giant spider. Why hadn't he mentioned it? Surely this sort of thing couldn't be common, not even in Ancient Greece.

Zoe echoed his thoughts. "Jason didn't tell us you're a … a …" She seemed reluctant to say the word.

"That's because he doesn't know! I was transformed months ago, and he hasn't got a clue. Humph. Shows how much he cares, the schmuck." Arachne quivered with indignation.

"So how …"

"Never cross the gods, that's all I can say. I happened to mention – just in passing – that I was a better weaver than the goddess Athena. She didn't like it. Truth hurts!" Arachne bristled and started to rear up. "So Athena challenged me to a contest. My work was clearly superior, but, that just made the goddess angry. She put a curse on me. 'Spin and weave forever,' she said. Then she turned me into this!"

If Athena was anything like Hera, then Tim wasn't surprised. He had seen how vindictive the gods could be first hand. "That's so unfair. Will she change you back?" he asked.

"I doubt it. But that's okay." Calming slightly, Arachne settled again. "I like being a spider. My weaving is better than ever! And I never get tired. The diet's not so great, but meh. Can't have everything."

Not too sure what her diet was, Tim slid farther away. Next to him, Zoe went rigid.

"You're frightened, aren't you? I knew you would be." Arachne's eight eyes glittered.

"Yes. No. Um." Tim decided to move the conversation along. "So, this favor we wanted to ask …" The spider remained silent so Tim kept talking. "Jason said he gave you the Golden Fleece. We'd like to borrow it if that's okay. Just for a little bit, and we'll bring it straight back. Promise."

"Well you could," Arachne said as Tim crossed his fingers, "if I hadn't unpicked it already."

Forgetting her fear of the giant spider, Zoe burst out, "Unpicked it! Are you crazy? Don't you know how precious the fleece is?"

"Settle down, little madam," Arachne warned, heaving her enormous body upward.

Tim recalled how frightened his mother had been when she saw the spider on the wall. She was convinced it would jump on them. Arachne was holding herself in the exact same way as that spider, legs stiff and back arched. Was she about to attack? Tim had never been afraid of spiders before, but looking at the quivering giant in front of him made him think again. He gripped the wooden bench.

"If you will let me explain, before jumping to conclusions." Arachne turned and scuttled across the courtyard, her multiple feet tip-tapping on the tiles.

Tim relaxed his grip. Spiders don't attack by walking away. Unless she was planning on giving herself a good long run-up before turning around and …

"Come along, I'll show you what I did to the fleece."

Tim and Zoe eyed each other nervously. "If she wants to hurt us, she would've by now," Tim said in a low voice. "Let's see what she wants." Zoe frowned but slid off the bench. The children walked across the courtyard, keeping clear of the web.

"This is my workshop," Arachne said, standing by an open doorway. "Look inside."

Rows and rows of shelves lined the walls. The shelves sagged under the weight of the woven items stacked on top of them: shawls, blankets, rugs. A wooden loom stood in the corner of the room, surrounded by dozens of balls of wool. They were all colors of the rainbow: brilliant blues, rich reds, and vibrant emerald greens. Dotted between them twinkled rare flashes of the purest gold. It had to be the fleece! Unpicked and spun into a fine thread.

"WOW,"

Zoe said, fingering some delicate lacework. Gossamer-fine, the strands were thinner than human hair and glowed with a pearly translucence. "I've never seen such beautiful work. No wonder Athena was jealous. You're the best."

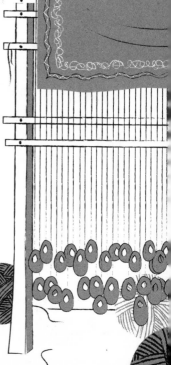

Arachne swelled with pride. "I know," she said, twitching happily. "Have a look around. See if anything takes your fancy. You won't find better quality anywhere."

A display stand caught Tim's eye. "FOR SALE" a sign said. "BUY ONE GET ONE FREE." An array of items was spread out, reminding Tim of the fancy department stores in London.

"Is this a shop?" he said in surprise.

"And why not?" Arachne replied. "Jason's not the only one to have a hobby! He has no business sense, though. I told him he could make a fortune selling those boats, but he didn't want to know. He'd rather keep them for himself." She opened and closed her mandibles in contempt.

"So you set up a shop?" Tim was still trying to get his head around the idea of a store-owning spider.

"I can't sit around waiting for Jason all my life! After I hadn't heard from him for so long, I decided to set up my own business. I do quite well out of it, if you must know."

"I'm sure you do," Tim hastened to say. "Everything's lovely."

"You're in luck, because I happen to have an exclusive fleece item for sale. Have a look at this stand here."

Tim examined the items; there was no mistaking that warm golden glow. But …

"Gloves? You turned the Golden Fleece into gloves?"

"Brilliant, isn't it? They'll keep you *miraculously* warm, that's my slogan. Would you like them? They're one of a kind. Five drachma. Buy the left glove, get the right one free."

Tim had a few pounds in his pocket, but didn't think Arachne would accept a currency that hadn't been invented yet. He looked questioningly at Zoe, who shook her head.

"We don't have any money," said Tim. "But could you please lend them to us? We won't damage them and we promise to bring them right back."

But Arachne was shaking her head. "I'd go out of business straight away if I carried on like that. Sorry, children." She fixed Tim with her eight-eyed glare. "If you want these gloves, you have to pay."

◾ ◾ ◾

"Can't you ask your dad?" Tim asked as they walked dejectedly away. "He might give you the money. Especially if you tell him what it's for."

"Are you joking? Dad thinks girls should sit in the house weaving all day and not ask for anything."

"Your mother, then?"

Zoe kicked a pebble, sending it skittering down the path. "If Dad says no, Mom will agree with him. Humph. Are your parents like that too?"

Tim looked away. He'd known Zoe would ask about his family sooner or later, and he hated talking about it. Taking a deep breath, he decided not to beat around the bush. Get it out and get it over with. "I don't have a father. He died."

Tim tensed, waiting for the awkward outpouring of sympathy that was the usual

reaction when he told people. But all Zoe did was hold his hand and squeeze it.

"You can borrow mine any time you like," she said.

Grateful, Tim squeezed her hand back.

"Oh, how cute." Hermes suddenly appeared in front of them, wings flapping gently. "But aren't you a bit young for that sort of thing?"

Tim released Zoe's hand as if it had given him an electric shock, but she didn't seem to notice his discomfort. She didn't waste words. "Where's the vase? We want it back."

Hermes held up his hands in surrender. "Course you can have it, soon as you like. I couldn't help noticing, though, that you're in a spot of bother. You need some cash, right?"

"How did you know?" Zoe demanded. "Were you spying on us?"

"You weren't exactly whispering," Hermes said, scratching his cheek. "But worry not. I can help you out. Don't tell Hera, though. She wouldn't like it." And he winked.

As if they would tell the goddess! "That's very kind of you—" Tim started to say, but Zoe yanked his arm hard.

Thrusting her lips near his ear, she whispered deafeningly. "Don't trust him! He might be trying to get us to do something illegal."

"TUT TUT,"

Hermes said. "As if I would! Honest enterprise, that's what I'm offering. I've got a job for you."

"It's not stealing, is it?" Zoe asked. "There's no way we'd do that!"

"Stealing? Certainly not." Hermes' golden curls bobbed with indignation. "I've heard you're good at cleaning. My temple's a mess. It needs a thorough going over. How about it?"

"Cleaning?" Tim's shoulders drooped. He'd had enough of housework to last a lifetime. Helping out at home was different – Mom worked two jobs and he had no choice. But here? This was meant to be an adventure! A chance to be a statue-saving hero, not a cleaner.

Before Tim could object, Zoe asked, "How much?"

"Five drachmas," Hermes replied. "I'm robbing myself, I know, but I'm in the mood to be generous today. Normally I wouldn't pay more than four, but I hear you need five for that greedy Arachne."

"Ten," Zoe said promptly.

"Are you crazy? Six."

"Ten."

"Eight."

"Ten."

"All right, ten!" Hermes shook his head and laughed. "You drive a hard bargain! I must be crazy, but I like you kids and want to help out."

"In advance." Zoe held out her hand.

"Done!" A few coins appeared in midair in front of the god. Hermes snatched at them, then handed them over with a bow.

Tim's eyes widened. What a good trick! If only he could do that, his family's money troubles would be over. Zoe passed the coins to Tim, who tucked them safely into his pants pocket.

"Excellent!" Hermes said. "You'll be wanting to get started."

Tim didn't want to get started, not at all, but he couldn't come up with an alternative. As they walked to Hermes' temple, the god described the chores. "Just a general tidying up will do. Sweep and mop. Dust the offerings and polish the statues. Wipe down the columns. Shampoo the sacrifices. You know, the basics."

Tim groaned. That would take all day! By the time they would be able to buy the Golden Fleece gloves, the sun would be setting. Although Stheno the gorgon was dead, Tim didn't fancy venturing into her garden at nighttime.

"Right," Hermes said as they approached his temple. Like Hera's, it was well maintained and colorful. It was smaller than the queen goddess' temple, for which Tim was grateful. It meant less cleaning. "You'll find the equipment in the back there. Be sure not to break anything – catch you later!" With that, the wings on Hermes' cap and sandals started to flap vigorously and the young god flew away.

As soon as he'd gone, Zoe darted to the antechamber. "Now's our chance! Can you see the vase anywhere?" she asked, hunting among the offerings.

Tim peered at a cluster of jugs and jars. Now that the fracture lines were gone, his vase looked a lot like the others, making it harder to spot. He was starting to think it wasn't there after all, until he saw the familiar drawing of Hercules wrestling the bull.

"It's here! See, Hera hasn't got it."

"Hmmm." Zoe almost sounded disappointed, as if she didn't like being proved wrong.

Tim handed Zoe a cleaning rag. "I told you, Hermes is on our side. When we've saved the statues, I'll ask him for the vase back. He said I could have it when I'm ready."

"And you believe him?"

Tim shrugged. "It's here, isn't it? He hasn't given it to Hera." Sighing, he picked up a broom and started sweeping.

Silence fell as the kids went about their tasks. Something was troubling Tim,

though, and it was more than just a dislike of cleaning. After a few minutes of vigorous sweeping, he decided to share his concern with Zoe. "Do you think the fleece will still work?" he asked, leaning on the broom handle. "I mean, it's been picked apart and turned into gloves. Maybe it's lost its magic."

"Don't say that." Frowning, Zoe ran her rag over a jug. "It's got to work." She continued dusting for a few moments, then voiced her own concerns. "I know you think Hermes is okay. But have you noticed how he always turns up? Odd, don't you think?"

"Probably coincidence," Tim said. He patted his pocket, checking that the coins were still there. They clinked reassuringly. "Without him, we'd have no hope."

Zoe opened her mouth to say more, but the sound of yowling birds made the words freeze on her lips.

THE PEACOCKS!

Tim yelped. How had they found him here, at Hermes' temple? Surely they only guarded Hera's domain.

"Now do you believe me?" Zoe said, dropping the cleaning rag.

"Quick, we have to go before–"

But it was too late. Hera's flock of peacocks materialized and circled around them, cutting off their exits. Before Tim had a chance to even blink, the queen goddess herself appeared, just inches away.

"GOT YOU!"

she crowed, grabbing Tim by his collar and lifting him into the air. Hera was surprisingly strong.

Zoe pushed the goddess roughly, making her stumble. "Let him go!"

"You will pay for that, brat of Hercules," the goddess hissed, recovering her balance. "But first – behold your friend." Hera lifted her free hand and clicked.

And then the strangest thing happened. Everything started getting bigger! The goddess, the temple. Even Zoe. All steadily growing to gigantic size. Zoe clapped her hand over her mouth and shrieked.

Her voice was loud and shrill, hurting Tim's ears. "Don't worry Tim, I'll save you," she boomed. "I'll find someone who can change you back."

Change him? Surely she was the one that needed help? It was then that he realized what must have happened. The world hadn't grown, he'd shrunk! His legs dangled in the air as Hera clutched him between her fingertips.

"Save him?" Hera laughed, her voice booming and echoing. "I don't think so. I trapped your father for 3,000 years. Timothy Baker will be trapped for thousands more!"

Tim pedaled his legs wildly as if he
were riding a bike. There was
nothing for his feet to grip
onto, though. Only thin air.
Hera's gigantic face loomed
closer as she lifted him
higher. Glinting with a cold
fire, her pale blue eyes looked
as big as truck tires as they
bored into his.

"Let this be a lesson to those who seek to disobey me," she hissed. The force of her breath made his hair flutter. "Timothy Baker, friend of Hercules, son of a distant land. The boy from the future. Except … let it be known to all that you no longer have a future. Into the cursed amphora you go. May you remain there for all eternity."

Tim heard Zoe scream, a loud, shrill sound that shook the molecules of air around him. Hera released her grip and he felt himself falling, spiraling downward. Sights flashed before his eyes one after the other. The elegant columns of Hermes' temple. Hera's triumphant smile. Zoe's horrified stare. And then –

darkness. A cloying, heavy blackness that surrounded him on all sides.

Before he had time to shout, Tim felt himself land. The ground was slippery and sloped up sharply on all sides. He reached out his hands. He could almost touch the walls on either side and a feeling of claustrophobia washed over him. Tim knew what had happened and where he was. Hercules' former prison was now *his* prison.

He could hear muffled voices arguing outside. He guessed it was Zoe and Hera, but the sounds were distant and hard to understand. Tim had to concentrate to make out the words.

"I'M GOING TO GET DAD!"

Zoe was shouting.

"Please do," Hera purred. "Tell him to come rescue his little friend."

"Don't do it!" Tim tried to shout out a warning, but his voice echoed oddly in the confined space: "Do it do it do it." He clapped his hand over his mouth. It wasn't meant to come out like that! He didn't want Hercules to be captured too. "Zoe, no!" he called out. "No no no no," went the echo. Tim realized he had to stop talking or he would miss too much of the conversation.

"I shall trap him as well," Hera was saying. "But worry not. At least your father will have company this time."

Tim could hear Zoe sobbing. His hands clenched into fists. There had to be a way out. He examined the walls of the vase. They were far too smooth. There were no hand or foot holds, no way for him to scale the walls that bulged outward then curved sharply inward. If only Hermes hadn't fixed the vase. The old fracture lines might have been enough for Tim to grip onto and scramble his way out. Tim's chest tightened as he wondered whether that had been on purpose. Had Hermes been in on Hera's plan to trap him? Or was it a coincidence that he'd decided to fix the vase?

A sudden jolt jarred his body and the world vibrated. A faint humming sound filled the air. Tim realized Hera must have put the vase down. He strained to hear what they were saying.

"I am leaving now," Hera said. "Do not even think of touching this vase. I am putting my fiercest peacock on guard. Now go, my child. Go

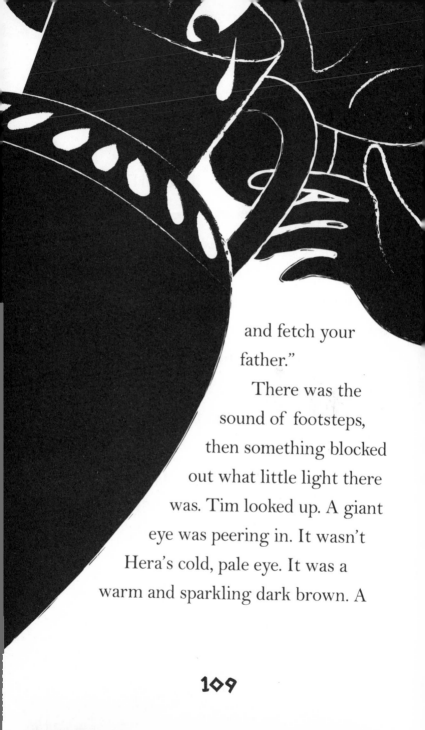

and fetch your father."

There was the sound of footsteps, then something blocked out what little light there was. Tim looked up. A giant eye was peering in. It wasn't Hera's cold, pale eye. It was a warm and sparkling dark brown. A tear welled up in the corner and trickled out. It had to be Zoe. Tim could hear the peacock growling as the little girl peered in.

"Don't touch the vase," Tim warned, "or you'll be attacked by the bird."

"I'm going to get help."

"Don't get your dad. We'll figure something out. There has to be a way."

"I'll ask Theseus to save you." Zoe was talking about the vain hero that had tried to help them out of the labyrinth they were once trapped in.

"He's not going to help," Tim called back. "He'll be too busy brushing his hair."

"My great-great-grandfather?"

Tim rubbed his face and groaned. "If Perseus sees this vase, he'll fill it with flowers."

"Who then?"

Tim didn't know. "Jason?"

Zoe snorted. "He won't even look up from his boat. I know. I'll ask my mother what to do."

"Don't! She might send your dad, and then he'll be trapped too. We have to figure this out ourselves."

Zoe was quiet for a moment. "What if I break it? You know, just knock it over and let it shatter."

Tim thought about it. It might work. Hercules had survived the vase being broken, but then again he was a demigod. Tim was just an ordinary boy. He didn't know what effect shattering the vase would have on him. And how would he get home without it? Still, what choice did they have? It was either take a chance or be stuck in the vase forever. "Try it. But, um, be gentle."

"Break it gently?" Although she was distressed, Zoe hadn't lost her sarcasm.

"All right, smash it. I'll just … brace … myself." Tim sat cross-legged on the floor and curled his arms protectively over his head. "Right," he called. "One. Two. Three.

NOW!"

But instead of feeling the vase topple over and smash, he heard a hideous growling, followed by a high-pitched scream. The peacock! "Zoe? Are you all right?"

After a few seconds her eye appeared

over the vase again. Her voice sounded shakier than ever. "I'm okay. That stupid bird flew at me, but I didn't touch the vase so it backed off. I'll go get help from … someone. Wait there."

Of course he'd wait. What else could he do? Tim heard Zoe's footsteps ringing across the temple floor. Cramped and uncomfortable, he closed his eyes.

And waited.

11

Ringlets streaming out behind her, Zoe left the vase where Hera had put it on the plinth. She ran from Hermes' temple down the paved path. There was only one person left that she could think of to approach. The very thought of asking the giant spider frightened and horrified Zoe, but she didn't know what else to do. She dared not expose her father to Hera's trap. Summoning up her courage, she

retraced her steps to Arachne's house.
She braced herself and knocked on the
front door.

This time, the giant spider flung the
door open instantly, as if she'd been

waiting for them. "You've brought the money for the gloves?" Arachne got straight to the point.

"Yeah-no. Yes. I mean no. Tim's got it." Zoe hated that she became so tongue-tied in the spider's presence. It would help if Arachne's eyes didn't glitter and gleam like that, as if she were imagining what the children tasted like.

"Five drachmas," Arachne said. "I don't haggle."

"Five is fine. But Tim's trapped! Hera put a curse on him and trapped him in a vase, and he can't get out."

Arachne opened and closed her mandibles thoughtfully. "Why did you come to me?"

"I – I hoped you might rescue him," Zoe said, taking a step backward. "So we can give you the money for the gloves."

The spider was quiet for a moment. She lifted her two front legs and Zoe nearly toppled over backward. Arachne was only smoothing down her apron. After some twitching and fidgeting, she said, "Ten drachmas."

"Excuse me?"

"Ten drachmas for the gloves. If you want my help."

Zoe agreed eagerly enough. They had the money. It was worth it!

"Wait here."

Zoe was relieved that she didn't have to enter Arachne's home again. She stood on the doorstep, jiggling with impatience, as the spider scuttled across the courtyard to her workshop. Before long Arachne emerged, the glowing pair of Golden Fleece gloves thrust into her apron pocket.

"Lead on."

Cringing at the sound of Arachne's feet tip-tapping on the path, Zoe darted to Hermes' temple as fast as she could. Hera's peacock was still standing guard over the vase. When it saw Zoe it growled.

"Tim, are you still there?" Zoe called, keeping her distance.

"Yes!" Tim replied, his voice faint and echoing. "Of course I am."

"I've brought Arachne. She'll get you out."

Silence. Then Zoe heard a soft *psst* sound, a bit like steam escaping from a volcanic fissure. It seemed to be coming from the vase. What did it mean? She walked closer, keeping a wary eye on the peacock. Zoe held her hands behind her back to show the aggressive bird that she

wasn't planning on touching anything. Another *psst* came from the vase, this time more forceful. Zoe leaned over and put her eye near the opening.

Tim was staring up at her. "Psst! Oh, you're here. Are you sure we can trust Arachne? I mean, I like spiders and all, but she's so big and I'm tiny! I feel like a fly waiting to be eaten."

Zoe put her lips near the vase opening and whispered, "I said we'd pay her ten drachmas. I don't think she'll eat you, she just wants her money." She pulled back to look at Tim again.

The miniature boy ran his hands through his curly mop of hair. "I hope you're right. Do you think she looks hungry?"

"Do you children want my help or not?" Arachne asked, running out of patience. "You promise me money, I come all the way here, and you two sit around whispering. I haven't got all day. Time is money."

"YES, PLEASE!"

Zoe said, backing away from the vase. "We want your help. Please rescue my friend."

"Humph." Arachne arched her back but said no more.

"What are you going to do?" Zoe wanted to know.

Arachne didn't reply. Instead, she started to tremble violently. Her entire body jerked and twitched, as if she were a puppet on strings. Wide-eyed, Zoe watched as Arachne grew even larger, before suddenly starting to shrink. Smaller and smaller, until she became the size of a rat. It was better than being human-sized, but even a rat-sized spider was way too big in Zoe's opinion.

Arachne scuttled along the temple floor and climbed up the plinth. Zoe watched the peacock warily to see if it would do anything. She wondered whether the colorful bird ate spiders, and part of her couldn't help hoping that it did. But it seemed that as long as Zoe didn't touch the vase herself, the bird was content to watch in peace.

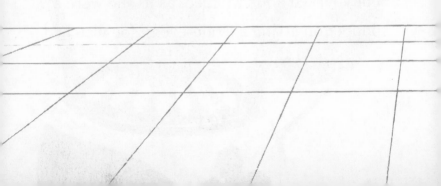

Arachne's slender legs crept over the surface of the vase in stealthy, slinking movements, making a skittering sound. Zoe shuddered. As Arachne climbed higher, the vase started to tilt. Her weight threatened to pull it over. It only stabilized when she reached the very top.

As if in celebration, Arachne arched her back and pointed her fangs to the sky. Drops of moisture glistened on their tips, looking suspiciously like venom. Arachne paused at the lip like a diver about to enter a pool, then plunged into the vase.

Tim watched as Arachne lowered herself toward him, spinning a thread that stretched down from the lip of the vase. She glided smoothly, like a paratrooper being lowered from a helicopter. Tim couldn't help feeling nervous. Even though the spider had shrunk herself to fit into the vase, she was still way bigger than he was.

"Hold still and don't wriggle," Arachne commanded as she loomed closer. "This won't hurt a bit."

Tim shuddered as he felt Arachne grip him with her hairy legs. Horrified, he felt himself being spun around and around. It made him dizzy, and images of meat being turned on a spit floated unpleasantly through his mind. Soon he was covered with Arachne's web. The strong, silky threads pinned his arms to his sides, encasing him all the way down to his ankles. Only his head and feet poked out. He tried to wriggle, but it was no use.

Tim felt like a caterpillar in a cocoon. Or was it more like an Egyptian mummy? Either way, he couldn't move a muscle.

"How's that? Comfy?" Arachne's eight eyes gleamed.

Tim gulped. "Um. Yes." He knew he was utterly at her mercy. If she decided to sink her fangs in, there was nothing he could do to save himself.

"You have the ten drachmas?"

"In my pocket."

She nodded. "Good. Hold on tight."

Arachne climbed
back up toward
the vase opening,
dragging Tim along
on the end of her
silken rope. The
rope swayed like a
pendulum, bumping
him against the walls.
It left Tim feeling
sore and bruised, but
he gritted his teeth and
didn't complain. No point
offending the touchy spider.
Finally they reached the top,
then suddenly Tim was flung
up and over, out into the open

air. He blinked, his eyes watering as they adjusted to the bright light.

"Are you ready for what comes next?" The spider was perched on one of the vase's handles. She peered down at Tim, who was dangling below her. The ground looked very far away.

Arachne's words sent a shudder down his spine. "Y-yes. I think so." He hoped she wasn't talking about eating him for lunch.

Lunging toward him, Arachne slashed downward with her fangs. Tim's shout of fear turned into one of surprise as he saw the web rope snap. She had sliced it and released him! He plunged to the ground, tumbling head over heels as he spun out of control.

"OOF."

Tim's breath was knocked out of him as he hit the floor, but luckily the thick silky cocoon cushioned his fall. He bounced a bit before coming to a complete stop.

Then the most incredible thing happened. The base of the vase seemed to be moving closer toward him, racing rapidly across the temple floor. Next thing he knew, the vase was shrinking away underneath him. Everything looked like it was moving closer and getting smaller at the same time. Tim knew what it meant. He was growing. Now that he was out of the vase, Hera's spell was reversing and he was going back to his normal size. The web strands turned from big glistening

ropes into tiny threads, and he brushed
them off his school jacket.

Laughing with relief, Tim twisted his
spine and stretched out his arms. This felt so
much better. He didn't know how Hercules
had stood it for so long. No wonder the hero
was delighted when he escaped!

"Hey, does that mean–" It crossed Tim's
mind that being in the vase might have
turned him invisible, just like it had with
Hercules.

Would he, too, only be visible to his rescuer — in this case, Arachne? That would be awful! Tim tried to imagine what life would be like if nobody could ever see him again. Everyone would feel sad and miss him, even if he was standing right next to them. His mother, his teachers. His best friend Ajay and his new friend Zoe.

Leo the bully …

Actually, that mightn't be too bad, Tim realized. He smiled as he thought of all the things he could get away with if Leo couldn't see him …

Deciding to test out his visibility, Tim made an ugly face and wiggled his hands under Zoe's nose.

"What are you doing?" She stared at him as if he'd lost his mind. "Are you feeling unwell? Did the vase do something to your brain?"

"Uh–" Tim guessed he wasn't invisible after all. He grinned sheepishly.

"Ten drachmas, please." Arachne had also gone back to her normal size. "Put them in my apron pocket and take the gloves. Oh – and you're welcome," she said pointedly.

"Thanks! I was about to say thank you, honest. It's just that I'm a bit … you know." Arachne gave Tim a stony look, so he stopped babbling. He dug the coins out of his pants pocket without further comment.

No longer afraid of the spider, he reached over and dropped the coins in her apron. He drew out the gloves and marveled. Tim had never felt anything like them before. Warm, soft, and silky, yet firm to the touch. The gloves even seemed to be vibrating gently. He held them to his ear and thought he could hear a gentle hum.

Tim folded them carefully and placed them in his jacket pocket. The gloves felt comfortingly toasty against his chest. Finally, they could try to save those poor statues.

"Let's go," he said to Zoe, "to the gorgon's garden!"

"Hooray!" Zoe clapped her hands together in delight. "But we'd better take the vase with us," she added, glancing at it warily. "When Hera comes back and discovers that you've escaped …"

"You're right." Tim had no desire to ever be trapped again. It had been the most frightening experience of his life, even worse than being lost in the labyrinth. He reached for the vase.

Zoe reminded him. "It'll call Hera."

Tim froze.

The bird twitched its head and raised its wings threateningly. Dashing between Tim and the vase, the peacock opened its beak. Ready to summon its mistress.

Fast as a whip, Arachne reared on her back legs and pointed her fangs at Hera's bird. "Don't even think about it," the giant spider hissed. "I haven't had my lunch yet, and pureed peacock is my favorite meal."

Whimpering like a frightened puppy, the bird turned tail and fled. It ran out of Hermes' temple, down the path, and disappeared from sight.

"Nice trick." Tim licked the beads of sweat that had broken out on his upper lip. "Thank you."

"You're welcome." Arachne lowered herself back onto all eight legs and turned to face him. "I wasn't lying, you know – I *am* very hungry. Puree of peacock is good, but kid casserole is also acceptable." Her eyes gleamed, and she edged closer.

"Ah …" Tim backed away, tensing himself to turn and run if necessary. He heard Zoe gasp, and he put a protective arm in front of her. "You wouldn't hurt us. You just saved my life. You didn't have to do that, did you? It shows you like us. Not in an eating way, that is." He thought he ought to clarify.

"Let me tell you something, little boy. Since being transformed, I don't just look like a spider. I think like one too. I told you before that children are scared of me. There's a good reason for that." She edged closer still and quivered.

"THEY'RE DELICIOUS!"

139

Tim gulped but said nothing. He was sifting through various options, trying to work out which way to run if the giant spider suddenly pounced on them.

"But business before pleasure, that's my motto." Arachne jiggled the coins in her apron. It was hard to read the spider's expression, but Tim thought she looked more smug than menacing.

He wasn't sure what was happening. Was she about to attack them or not?

"Ten drachmas, excellent," Arachne continued, her body bobbing up and down. "Thank you for your business. Come again for all your shawls, chitons, rugs, and other woven goods. Best price and quality guaranteed. Be sure to tell your friends!"

"W-we will," Tim stammered. *I'll tell them to stay away*, he thought, but he didn't say it.

"I'm off to get someone for lunch now. Goodbye."

Tim and Zoe stood motionless as they watched Arachne turn and scuttle away, her hairy legs scraping across the floor tiles.

"Oh my gods," breathed Zoe. "That was the scariest thing ever. I was right about her." She shook herself, as if trying to get back to her senses. "We'd better get out of here. If that bird summons Hera–"

"You're right. Help me with the vase. Hurry!"

The two children held it between them and started on the long journey to the gorgon's garden. Tim wished there was somewhere safe to leave the heavy object, but it was too risky. If he left it at Hermes' temple, Hera would get it. If they went to Zoe's house, Hercules might ground them. There was no way he could ask Arachne to mind it. And Jason? He'd throw it in the ocean to see if it floated like a boat.

Tim found it strange to be holding the object that had been his prison such a short time ago. To think, he might have been trapped in there forever. Maybe even ending up on his own mantelpiece, with his mother having no idea he was inside!

"How come I'm not invisible?" Tim wondered out loud. "Your dad was when he escaped from the vase."

Zoe shrugged. "Hera must have said a different curse when she trapped him. I can see why. She wouldn't want Dad to become a hero again if he ever got out. Making him invisible would have stopped that."

Tim nodded. It made sense. If Hercules went around being brave and saving people in the modern world, he'd have become a celebrity. He'd have gone on reality TV shows and everyone would have praised him. Hera wouldn't be able to stand that. She obviously had no concerns about Tim ever becoming a famous hero, so she hadn't bothered to make him invisible.

"Lucky Dad's back to normal now," Zoe said with feeling. "Or he'd be always checking up on me – and I wouldn't even know it!"

"So when I solved the riddle, Hera's spell reversed." Tim chuckled as he thought it through. "And now everyone can see him again. No wonder she's cross."

Zoe threw her ringlets back and laughed.

■　■　■

Finally, after some hard walking, the children reached the edge of the gorgon's garden. Tim looked around. Apart from the statues, the place looked deserted.

"How many gorgons did your great-great-grandad say there were?" Tim wanted to check before getting any closer.

"Three," Zoe replied. "He killed one. Theseus killed another." She eased the vase to the ground and rolled her shoulders.

"So there's one left?" Tim glanced around anxiously, but all he could see were rows and rows of flowers.

"Oh yes. But don't worry. She doesn't live here."

"Are you sure?"

"Fairly sure. Grandpa would have said something."

"Mmm." Tim didn't feel too confident. Perseus wasn't likely to concern himself about another gorgon unless she turned his plants to stone.

"We can ask him. Here he comes."

"Grandad," Zoe called out to the hobbling old man. "Is the last gorgon here?"

"Euryale? I should say not. No sense of beauty, that one. She has no interest in flowers whatsoever, not like her sister." Perseus sniffed and looked at the children. "You took your time. Did you get the Golden Fleece?"

"Sort of." Tim drew the gloves out of his pocket. "It ended up as these."

Perseus' gray eyebrows shot up his creased forehead. "How are they going to work now?" he grumbled. "I can't see these curing my marigold mildew. All these are good for is playing dress-up!"

"Do you think so?" Tim was worried. He suspected Perseus was right. Maybe the fleece wouldn't work, not now that it had been changed so much.

"Only one way to find out," Zoe said. "LET'S TRY IT."

"I was going to drape the fleece delicately over the flower bed." Perseus scowled, his hands miming the actions. "Now what do I do? Dress the flowers up like little humans? Maybe you can bring me some tiny sandals and chitons, too!"

"I meant the statues." Zoe nodded at Tim. "Go put them on one."

Tim turned to the nearest figure. It was a pretty young woman, her long hair in elaborate braids. Tears trickled down her cheeks. "I'm here to help." Tim peered into her stony eyes. "Don't worry. This'll make you good as new."

At least he hoped so.

Tim stretched one of the gloves over the statue's hand. It was harder than it looked. The fingers were stiff and unmoving, bent at sharp angles. Tim was worried that he might accidentally tear the gloves but they were surprisingly strong. Biting his lip, he twisted and poked

and tugged. Finally it was done. He put
the second glove on her other hand. The
crying statue was wearing the Golden
Fleece gloves.

But would they work?

Tim stood back, watching.
Glad that his fingers
weren't made of stone,
he crossed them.

14

At first it looked like nothing was happening. The statue remained hunched over, as solid and unmoving as ever. The only difference was that it now sported a nifty pair of golden gloves.

Tim sighed. After all he'd been through – getting trapped in a vase and then nearly being eaten by an oversize arachnid – his plan had failed. Maybe Arachne's actions had made the Golden Fleece lose its magical properties after all. Or maybe it never had any to begin with, and the whole thing was only a myth. Either way, there was no point in brooding. He'd just have to come up with another idea.

"Tim!" Zoe nudged him with her elbow.

"I know, I'm sorry. But never mind, we'll think of something else."

"No, silly, look! Look at her wrists."

"Wha–?" Tim followed Zoe's gaze and the question died on his lips.

The statue's wrists did indeed look different. They had lost some of their grayness. Ever so slowly, they were turning the healthy color of flesh. As the children watched, the color crept up the statue's arms, gradually at first but picking up speed. It spread to her shoulders, her throat, then raced across her whole body. The young woman's frozen look of horror turned to one of sheer joy.

"My hero! I was stuck for years, cold and tired and miserable. And now I'm free! Thank you so much!" Laughing, she flung her arms around Tim and kissed him loudly on the cheek. Heat flooded Tim's face and he pulled away. "Y-you're welcome," he stammered, feeling thrilled and

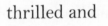

embarrassed at the same time. "Can I have the gloves back, please?" He waved his hand at the other statues. "We have to help them too."

"Of course." Bouncing with joy, the woman peeled off the gloves and held them out.

Tim tensed, hoping that removing the fleece wouldn't make her freeze up again. It didn't. His smile grew broader.

Tim and Zoe went from statue to statue, putting on the gloves then standing back to watch the miracle unfold. It took a long time to rescue all the crying statues – there were so many of them – but it was worth it. Their gratitude and delight made a few tears trickle down Tim's cheeks too.

"Hah, well done! Good girl, Zoe."
Perseus was watching from the shade of
a flowering tree. The old man smiled at
the children before starting to squawk,
"Hey, don't step in those flower beds.

NO – BE CAREFUL!"

Perseus hobbled around,
scowling at the liberated gorgon

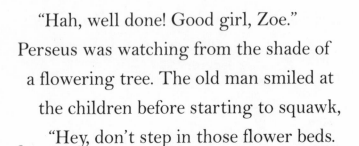

victims. He shook
his walking stick
at them as they
capered about. Some
were dancing. Others
were doing backflips
and cartwheels. One of
the gorgon's victims had
been frozen while holding
a stringed instrument
that looked like a cross
between a guitar and a
harp. He started to
play and everyone
whooped with
pleasure.

"Party time!" A girl grabbed a fistful of blossoms and tossed them in the air. "Woohoo!"

"Stop! No!" Perseus scolded. "It took me hours to plant those. Go away! Everyone back to your houses, shoo!"

The gorgon's victims started to dance in an erratic circle, feet stamping and kicking. The circle weaved in and out of the rows of flowers. Tim and Zoe looked at each other, nodded, and joined the circle of dancers.

■ ■ ■

"Zoe!" The loud voice boomed across the garden. "I have found you at last."

The voice was familiar, but the expression on the tall man's face was not. It was Hercules, legs apart, arms folded.

But rather than the usual friendly sparkle, the hero was smoldering like an ember about to burst into flames.

"Daddy." Zoe broke away from the circle and skipped toward him. "We saved the gorgon's statues! Look, they're all people again. Isn't it wonderful?"

"Wonderful? I call it reckless. Girls should not go on quests! You might have been hurt." Hercules stamped his foot and the ground shook. It felt like a minor earthquake. The musician stopped playing and the dancers stopped leaping. Everybody stood and stared at the angry demigod.

"That's better," said Perseus, poking at a particularly energetic reveler with his walking stick. "Keep off my flowers."

"And you! Old man! How could you encourage such stupidity?"

Perseus fixed his great-grandson with a watery gaze. "Nice of you to visit me again. Only took you forty years."

Hercules was not about to go off-topic. "You are the one who said they should retrieve the Golden Fleece." He pointed an accusing finger at his ancestor. "Oh yes. I know all about it."

"So what if it was? Children need adventures."

Hercules quivered with rage. "They. Do. Not." He turned his gaze on Tim.

Tim smiled warily, waiting for the hero to smile back. He didn't.

"And you, Tim Baker." Hercules fell

silent, as if he were struggling with what he had to say.

"We were just trying to help," Tim said. "I wouldn't put Zoe in danger, honest."

"You could have saved her, could you?" All the friendliness had left Hercules' face. "If Arachne had tried to eat her while you were stuck in the vase? I know exactly what happened."

Tim turned a pebble with his shoe and couldn't meet the hero's eyes.

"It was all over the GGG." Hercules referred to the Greek God Grapevine, a system where gods could pass messages to heroes. "Hermes put out the warning, and let me tell you, all the grapes turned red!" It was red for danger, Tim recalled.

"I am sorry to do this, Tim Baker," Hercules added, his face grave. "I will never forget what you did for me. I will always consider you a true friend. But after what has happened … you cannot come back again."

"DAD, YOU CAN'T!"

Hercules continued as if his daughter hadn't spoken. "I am confiscating the vase."

Tim felt the blood drain from his face. He felt awful to have upset his friend so much. Tim remembered how kind Hercules had been to him. How he had offered to help with the housework. How he had kept trying to protect him. How he had encouraged him to stand up to Leo. And now he was looking at him through eyes as hard as flint.

"I didn't mean to upset you. I would never do anything to hurt Zoe!"

"I know you wouldn't, not on purpose." The hero's voice softened slightly. "But my first duty is to protect my daughter. I am sorry, my friend."

"But how will I get home?" Without the vase, Tim was stuck in Ancient

Greece. He liked it there, but not enough to give up his home.

"Hermes shall take you."

"You can't trust him," Zoe cried, wringing her hands together. "He'll hand Tim straight over to Hera. She can't wait to trap him again."

"Hermes has given his word to take him straight home. I, for one, trust the god." Hercules took a deep breath, as if his words pained him. "He will be here any minute now. I am sorry, Tim Baker. I have enjoyed seeing you again – but this is where it ends."

"Cheer up, Tim Baker." Hermes put Tim gently on the floor and grinned at him. They were standing in Tim's bedroom. The journey from Ancient Greece had been all too swift, his goodbyes all too brief. Tim's head drooped. Never again would he be able to travel to the past to see his friends. His adventures were over – and it was all his fault. If he hadn't put Zoe in danger, Hercules would never have confiscated the vase.

Tim blinked and a tear dribbled out. "I'm not sad," he said, wiping it away roughly. "The wind made my eyes water. That's all."

"Sure it did." Hermes nodded and the wings on his cap bobbed up and down. "So … you're not upset. In fact you're delighted, is that right?" He peered into Tim's face.

"Not exactly," Tim admitted. He thought he saw sympathy in the messenger god's eyes. Tim felt confused. Was Hermes on his side or on Hera's? He didn't know. Not that it mattered anymore. Tim sighed.

"You'd like to go back?"

"Of course I would. I don't want Hercules to be angry with me. I wish–" He sighed again, more heavily this time.

"You wish you still had the vase?"

"Yeah. But what's the point? Wishing doesn't make things happen." Tim had faced that sad fact a long time ago.

"Is that so?" Hermes tilted his cap at a cocky angle. "Then I guess there's no point in wishing for this!" And he clicked his fingers.

Tim's eyes bulged. He stared at what Hermes was suddenly holding in his hands.

"The vase! But-but, huh?" Tongue-tied, Tim lapsed into silence.

"Don't you want it? I can take it away again if you like."

"No! I want it. But how did you do that? Hercules took it." Tim barely dared to hope. "Did he change his mind?"

"I gave him a copy. A fake." Hermes winked. "This is the real vase, the magic one. He doesn't know the difference."

Tim felt torn. It was wrong to fool the hero like that. He didn't like the thought of his friend being tricked. But then again, without the vase he could never go back.

Maybe if Tim kept the vase ... If he went back and apologized ... If he told Hercules the truth ... If he did something helpful ... Maybe he could win Hercules' friendship again! Or would going back make things worse?

Hermes seemed to read the doubt in Tim's face. "Well if you don't want it …" The god sounded offended.

"I don't know–" A flurry of footsteps interrupted them. Tim's doorknob turned and the door squeaked open. Quick as a flash Hermes vanished, leaving the vase at Tim's feet.

"I came back to tell you I've made a decision," Mom said, poking her head in the room. "About … ah … about what I was talking about before. You know. The important thing."

"Uh huh." What should he do? Should he use the vase or was that a betrayal of trust?

"Tim. Are you listening to me?"

He jumped guiltily. "Yeah, sure. It's about …" It wasn't easy to drag his mind back to their conversation. Although it was only a few minutes ago for his mother, it was hours ago for him. So much had happened since then. Then it hit him. "Oh, you mean the central heating! Your face was red from the heat …"

Mom's cheeks went pink again. Evidently it was still acting up. "That's not it. I've decided to make a special dinner tonight." Mom looked at him expectantly. "Aren't you going to ask why?" she added when Tim didn't reply.

Tim blinked. He had to pay attention, even though a dinner didn't sound so exciting to him. "Err, yes. Why–?"

"Because we're having a special visitor!" Mom jumped in before he could finish. Her eyes sparkled with excitement.

Tim could tell she wanted him to ask more questions. He tried to put his dilemma out of his mind and focus. "Who is it? Grandma?" No one else sprung to mind.

"No." Mom shook her head and giggled. She sounded surprisingly like a schoolgirl. "Not Grandma. Oh, that reminds me. Don't forget to wear your gloves. Put them on now."

Without thinking, Tim reached into his jacket pocket. With so much on his mind, he'd forgotten he'd given the gloves his grandmother had knitted to Leo. Instead, he pulled out the Golden Fleece ones. Soft as silk, they glimmered and shone in his hands.

"Whoa – what happened to those?" Mom asked, her eyes widening. "They look amazing!"

"It's, um, just the light," Tim said, shoving them back into his pocket. He must have put them there after rescuing the statues and then forgotten all about it. He felt the gloves snuggled warmly against his chest. At least he had something to remind him of his adventure.

"But ..." Mom didn't look convinced.

"So who's coming to dinner?" Tim thought it best to change the subject.

"It's a surprise. You'll see." Mom giggled again.

■　■　■

Time passed slowly all day long. Tim tried to concentrate in class, but kept being distracted. Should he use the vase or shouldn't he? Who was the mystery dinner guest? The questions battled for his attention, winning out over spelling and long division.

Tim barely even noticed that Leo wasn't taunting him. Normally Leo took every chance to tease Tim, but today he'd backed off. Tim only realized that after he spotted Leo wearing the gloves. Was it possible for bullies to be silenced by kindness? Tim shook his head in disbelief. It was another of those wishes that rarely came true.

Mom came home early that evening. She set the dining table with their best plates. What with the napkins and crystal glasses, it almost looked like Christmas. All that was missing was the tinsel. And as for her makeup … Tim hadn't seen her wear any in years. And now she was all done up, dressed in her favorite dress. What was going on?

"Who did you say was coming?" Tim asked, narrowing his eyes at his mother. Her face lit up in a smile, and she looked years younger.

"I didn't say. But I hope you'll get along." Mom licked her finger and removed a smudge from Tim's cheek. "Be on your best behavior. I don't want any more talk of heroes and monsters."

Tim didn't think he talked about Ancient Greece that much. He made a mental note to be more careful in the future … if he ever went back again, that is.

"SO WHO IS IT?"

"It's a surprise. It's someone you know. Someone … nice."

Tim peered at her and frowned. Something was going on. Something he wasn't sure he'd like.

Mom jumped when the doorbell rang. "He's here! How do I look?" She patted her hair anxiously.

"You look great, Mom." Tim meant it. His mother was glowing with happiness, something he hadn't seen for years.

"Thank you, dear." She stooped down to give Tim a big hug. "I hope you like him. I know he likes you. I hope …" The doorbell rang again, and she rushed to answer the door.

Tim heard a man's voice. It was oddly familiar. It wasn't just the Australian accent that he recognized. He knew the voice, but couldn't quite place it. Tim shifted awkwardly from one foot to the other as he waited by the dining table.

A tall man breezed into the room. He walked straight up to Tim and ruffled his hair. "Good to see you, mate. How are you doing?"

Tim's jaw dropped. Standing in front of him, in his own house, was a teacher from his school! Tim had never been taught by him, but often saw him on the playground. Mom was holding a big bunch of roses that he must have given her. Her cheeks were as pink as the buds. Both adults wore shy, silly grins.

"Mr. Green," Tim squeaked.

"Please," Mr. Green said. "Call me Larry. We're going to see a lot of each other in the future, I hope."

Blinking rapidly, Tim looked from his mother to the teacher. They liked each other!

YUCK! Mom and Mr. Green ... Mr. Green and Mom ... Tim tried the words out in his head, but they didn't make any sense.

Tim still didn't know what to do about the past – and now the future was unclear too. Life was becoming more uncertain than ever.

Look out for Tim's next ADVENTURE!

~~*HOPELESS HEROES~~

PROBLEMS WITH
PYTHAGORAS!

STELLA
TARAKSON

Sweet
Cherry
PUBLISHING

"I've got the results of last week's math test." Miss Omiros picked a sheaf of papers off her desk and strode around the classroom, her high heels tapping. "Most people did well. Ajay came first as usual. Full credit, well done." The teacher smiled as she handed Ajay his test paper.

From across the room, Tim glimpsed a gigantic A written in red. He gave his best friend a thumbs up. Ajay suppressed a grin. He tried to look modest, but by the way his dark eyes gleamed, Tim knew he was feeling smug.

"Leo had the biggest improvement." Miss Omiros walked toward Tim's desk, which he unfortunately shared with his worst enemy, Leo the bully. Miss Omiros thought that making Leo sit closer to the front would improve his behavior. As if! She handed Leo his test paper, which had a big C written on it. "An improvement from last time. Keep up the good work."

Leo usually looked stone-faced when he got his marks, but now his pale lips twitched into a smile. It transformed his bull-like features into something almost human.

Miss Omiros paused in front of Tim. "So … what happened there? This isn't like you." Frowning, she handed over his paper.

Tim's eyebrows shot to the top of his forehead as he glanced at his mark.

An F.

F! A flood of heat rushed into his cheeks. Sure, math wasn't his best subject, but he usually did well enough. In his whole life, he'd never, ever–

"HAH! LOSER!"

Leo crowed gleefully as soon as the teacher moved on. "Who's the smart one now, Cinderella?"

Wincing at the sound of his nickname, Tim flipped the paper over with a snap, hiding the mark. He hated being called Cinderella. Just because he did the housework. He couldn't help it: Mom worked two jobs, and he was expected to help out. And now this!

"I had a bad day. That's all." Tim shrugged as if he didn't care.

"I beat you. You probably came last."

"Leo, that's enough," Miss Omiros said from across the room. "Don't spoil a good day by being unpleasant."

The bully fell silent, but he leered as he made a giant L with his thumb and forefinger and held it against his freckled forehead.

L for loser. F for failure. Tim felt a prickle in the corners of his eyes and blinked. He knew why his grades were bad. He hadn't concentrated during the test. His mind was too full. What with his friend Hercules being upset with him, and with Mr. Green turning out to be Mom's boyfriend …

It was all too much.

Tim still hadn't recovered from the shock of discovering that a teacher at his school was seeing Mom. Not that he disliked Mr. Green – or Larry, as he was told to call him. A laid-back Australian, most kids considered him cool. But it's one thing to chat with a teacher on the playground, and quite another to have him sitting in your kitchen making goo-goo eyes at your mother.

The getting-to-know-each-other dinner last week had been awkward. Tim hadn't wanted to say the wrong thing, so he'd said very little. Mom had kept flashing him anxious looks. It was clear she wanted everyone to get along. Tim tried to smile and act happy, but he'd still been reeling

from the fallout of his latest adventure in
Ancient Greece. Tim had returned to his
own time … in disgrace. Although he'd
looked regretful, Hercules had ordered
Tim to go home and never return.

Tim hadn't meant to put the hero's
daughter in danger! He and Zoe
had decided to rescue
a gorgon's victims –
people who'd been
turned to stone by
the monster's
glance. They'd
succeeded, but
Hercules had
banned Zoe
from going

on adventures ever
again. He'd even
confiscated the

MAGIC VASE

that allowed Tim to
travel through time.
Tim understood.
Hercules was only trying
to protect Zoe. It still hurt,
though.

Forcing the feeling from his
mind, Tim frowned at his math paper.
Where had he gone wrong? Numbers
swam before his eyes, blurring and
bumping into each other. They refused to
make sense. He needed help.

An idea struck, and he sat up straight. He could ask Mr. Gr– Larry! Everyone said the teacher was a math whiz. Then Tim could tell Mom that they were getting along well, and she'd be relieved. He'd kill two birds with one stone: help with math and a happy mother!

The bell rang and everyone jumped up, scraping their chairs against the floor. Tim spotted Larry on the playground, surrounded by a group of children.

Tim hadn't spoken to him since the night of the dinner, unsure what he should say to the man. A school trip to the British Museum was coming up, and Larry was one of the teachers that would be going. Tim had been worried that it would be awkward, but now he felt as if the problem were solved. He ran up to him and grinned shyly. The teacher smiled back.

"Hi Mr. … err … Larry."

The kids giggled when they heard him use the teacher's first name.

The smile froze on the man's face. "Not here," he muttered so that only Tim could hear. "Don't call me Larry here."

"Sorry! I meant Mr. Green."

"That's better. What can I do for you, mate?" The teacher sounded friendly, but he was talking to Tim like he would to any other kid in the school.

"Well, um …" Tim looked at the sea of faces, suddenly uncertain. Maybe this wasn't such a good idea. Were Mom and Mr. Green meant to be a secret? He vaguely recalled her saying that, but he'd been too busy fretting about Hercules to pay much attention.

"Yes?"

Tim had to be careful not to mention his mother. "I was hoping you'd help me with my math."

Mr. Green squinted down at him. "Is there any reason your teacher can't help? Miss Omiros, isn't it?"

"Yes. But I got a bad grade on my test and—"

"Sorry, mate. I'm sure Miss Omiros will help you."

The children looked at Tim as if he'd sprouted an extra head. Confused, he turned away, shoulders slumped. That hadn't gone well. Maybe talking to Mr. Green at school was a mistake. But how was he supposed to treat him? Like a friend or like a stranger? And shouldn't

Mr. Green *want* to help him? The teacher was coming over for dinner tonight, too. What if he told Mom about Tim's request for help? What if Mom got cross at Tim?

NOTHING WAS SIMPLE ANYMORE!

If only he had someone to talk to, someone who could tell him what stepfathers were meant to be like. He didn't want to upset Mom by complaining about Larry. And he couldn't tell Ajay, not if the relationship was meant to be a secret. The only person he could confide in lived thousands of years ago, in Ancient Greece. And Tim wasn't supposed to be able to go back.

Except … thanks to a trick played on Hercules by the god Hermes, Tim actually *could* go back if he wanted to. The question was: Should he?

Or would that make things worse?

Tim wasn't too sure about Hermes.
Could the messenger god – who was
also the god of thieves and liars
– be trusted? Unknown to
Hercules, Hermes
had swapped the
confiscated vase
with a fake copy. It
looked exactly the
same, but it had no

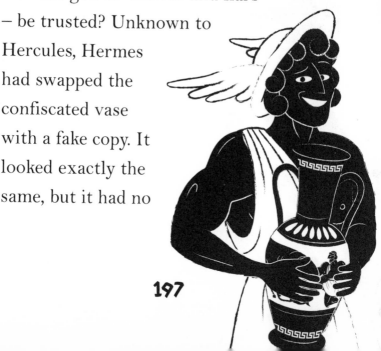

powers. He gave Hercules the copy and gave the magical vase back to Tim. He told Tim to use it to return to Ancient Greece whenever he liked.

So maybe the god was trying to be nice.

OR DID HE HAVE ANOTHER MOTIVE?

Hermes served Hera, Hercules' deadliest enemy. With a hatred born of jealousy, the angry goddess had once trapped the hero inside the magic vase. It was only when Tim

198

accidentally broke
the vase that the hero was
set free. Did Hera want Tim
to have the vase so that
she could use him to trap
Hercules again? It would be a
lot harder for her to take it from the
hero himself, Tim guessed. Hercules
would – hopefully! – take precautions.

All week long, Tim had felt torn.
Should he go back to Ancient Greece or
shouldn't he? Would Hercules accept his
apology or refuse to see him? If only
Larry– Mr. Green … had turned out to be
nicer. He might have been someone to go
to for advice. But no. The teacher couldn't

even be bothered to help Tim with math. It showed how much he cared!

Dinner that night turned out to be even more awkward than the first time. At least Mr. Green – who, confusingly, was now to be called Larry again – hadn't mentioned Tim's request for help. Not yet, anyway.

Tim picked at his food.

His mother asked him what was wrong.

"Don't you like your roast, dear? Usually you ask for seconds."

"I'm not hungry." Tim pushed the parsnip around his plate. He remembered how ravenous Hercules always seemed to be, and sighed.

"Not hungry? Are you feeling sick?"

"A bit," he admitted. He was. In a way.

❖❖

Mom leaned over and placed
a cool hand on his forehead.
"You don't have a fever. Maybe
something you ate disagreed with
you."

Tim started to nod, but froze when
Larry spoke.

"Or is something upsetting you?"

You are, is what Tim felt like saying, but didn't. Instead, he shrugged.

"Is there something wrong?" Mom asked, glancing from her boyfriend to her son.

"I – I failed my math test." Tim avoided looking at Larry.

"Really? That's not like you!" Mom's face creased with concern.

The teacher patted Tim on the shoulder. "No worries, mate. Everyone fails sometimes. Work harder and you'll be all right."

"Can't you help him, Larry? Math is your forté." Head tilted to the side, Mom gave her boyfriend a beaming smile. "I'm sure Tim will be grateful."

Larry shook his head. "I don't think it's right. It'd be favoritism."

Mom's smile faded and her eyes lost some of their shine. "It's hardly favoritism. You're not his teacher, so how can it be? All I'm saying is spend a few minutes going over what he got wrong. No one will know."

"I'll know," Larry said. "Tim will know. We should start as we mean to go on."

"So this is how you plan to go on! By ignoring my son when he has a problem!"

Uh oh. Now they were starting to fight. Because of him.

"Look, Penny, I think you're making too big a deal of this."

Mom's eyes flashed. "Is that so? I'm sorry that you feel that way!"

Whimpering, Tim pushed back his chair. Could things get any worse? He got up from the table and fled to his room, Mom's voice ringing in his ears.

. . .

Tim opened his wardrobe door and pulled out the vase. It was still draped in a sheet, even though there was no longer a need to keep it hidden. Not from Hermes, anyway. If the messenger god wanted to steal the vase, he wouldn't have given it to Tim in the first place. Even so, Tim didn't want Mom to see it. She'd only start asking awkward questions about its appearance. Last time Tim was in Greece, Hermes had magically fixed all the cracks that had criss-crossed over the vase. Now it looked as good as new.

Blinking furiously, Tim stared at the vase. He was so tempted to go back. Maybe Hercules had reconsidered the banishment. He might be missing Tim and feeling bad about things. Zoe would be.

If Tim went back, he could talk to the hero about Larry. Hercules was a good father. He would know what to do.

Mom's footsteps came pattering up the stairs. A second, heavier set of footsteps followed. Any moment now they'd burst into his room. They'd want to talk to him. Tim couldn't face it. Not yet. But would the vase even work? Maybe Hermes had lied and this one was the fake!

Tim's brain was in turmoil. It didn't know what to do, so it let his body decide.

His hands clasped the vase. They held on tight. As if from a distance, Tim heard his own voice squeak out, "Oh vase, take me to Zoe's house."

The next thing he knew he was flying through the air, golden sparks shimmering around him.

HOPELESS HEROES

To download Hopeless Heroes

ACTIVITIES
AND
POSTERS

visit:
www.sweetcherrypublishing.com/resources

Sweet
Cherry
PUBLISHING